Paulino

LONGMAN CLASSICS

Kidnapped

Robert Louis Stevenson

Simplified by D K Swan

Longman

Longman Group UK Limited,
Longman House, Burnt Mill, Harlow,
Essex CM20 2JE, England
and Associated Companies throughout the world.

This simplified edition © Longman Group UK Limited 1988

First published 1988

ISBN 0-582-01383-6

Set in 12/14 point Linotron 202 Versailles
Produced by Longman Group (FE) Limited
Printed in Hong Kong

Acknowledgements

Photographs © HTV for pages 8, 40, 48 and the cover; Transworld features for page 25 (David McCallum as Alan Breck), (background of sea and sky by The Image Bank); TV Times/ Transworld for pages 53 and 57.

The cover background is a wallpaper design called NUAGE, courtesy of Osborne and Little plc.

Stage 2: 900 word vocabulary

Please look under *New words* at the back of this book for explanations of words outside this stage.

Contents

Introduction

1	The house of Shaws	1
2	My uncle	6
3	The ship	12
4	To sea	18
5	The roundhouse	22
6	We hold the roundhouse	30
7	I hear about the "Red Fox"	34
8	We strike rocks	38
9	The lad with the silver button	42
10	The "Red Fox" dies	46
11	James of the Glens	51
12	In the heather	56
13	The lawyer	61
14	Shaws is mine	65
	Questions	67
	New words	71

Introduction

Robert Louis Stevenson

Robert Louis Stevenson was born in Edinburgh in Scotland in 1850. He had to end his college studies because his health was poor. He began to travel, looking for a place that was good for his health. An he wrote about his travels. *An Inland Voyage* (1878) was about journeys by canoe on the rivers and canals of Belgium and France. *Travels with a Donkey in the Cévennes* followed it in 1879.

People loved his travel books, and they also found his poems beautiful. In 1879 he travelled to California in a very uncomfortable ship (which may have been rather like the *Covenant* in this book) and then by train across the United States to San Francisco. He married in California, but his poor health made him and his wife travel again.

Readers of his travel books and poetry were surprised when *Treasure Island* came out in 1883. It was not at all like his earlier writing, but both children and grown-ups loved it.

Treasure Island was finished in Switzerland. Stevenson then continued to travel. He loved the islands of the southern Pacific Ocean, and he found that his health was better there. In the end, he and his wife made their home in Samoa. It was there that he wrote *Kidnapped* (1886), the story of David Balfour and Alan Breck. It was followed (but not immediately) by *Catriona* (1893), which continues the story of David Balfour and tells of other exciting adventures of David and Alan, and of David's love for Catriona Drummond. In between the two stories about David Balfour came another suprising book, the "thriller" called *The Strange Case of Dr Jekyll and Mr Hyde* (1886).

Stevenson died in Samoa in 1894, and he is buried there.

The history
The happenings, and even some of the people, in this story are not all imaginary.

When Queen Elizabeth I died without children in 1603, the person with best right to be the king of England was already the king of Scotland. So King James Stuart VI of Scotland became King James I of England. He was the first of a line of kings of England, Scotland and Ireland, the house of Stuart (or, as it is spelt in this book, Stewart). The last of the Stuart kings was James II. He was a Catholic, and he believed in a king's right to rule without Parliament. When a son was born in 1688, the thought of a continued line of Stuart kings displeased the English people, most of them non-Catholic and not believers in the "God-given" right of kings. They made him leave the country in 1688. Two non-Catholic daughters of James II ruled after him, but in 1714 there were no non-Catholics of the Stuart family, and the people with power in England – the "Whigs" – invited George, Elector of Hanover, a grandson of James I, to become King George I of England, Scotland and Ireland. When he died in 1727, his son became George II.

But there were a lot of people in the three countries, most of all in Scotland and Ireland, who wanted the Stuart line to continue. These "Jacobites" fought for James in Ireland in 1690 but were beaten. They fought for his son James Francis Edward Stuart in 1715 and were successful for a time in the Highlands of Scotland, but were again beaten.

Thirty years later, in 1745, the clans rose once more to fight, with other Jacobites, for Charles Edward Stuart, "Bonny Prince Charlie". They beat the English at Prestonpans outside Edinburgh and fought their way down into England. Charles waited at Derby for promised English and French help, but it did not come, and he had to return to Scotland. At Culloden, outside Inverness, the clansmen were beaten by the redcoats, horsemen and heavy guns of King George's army, and Bonny Prince Charlie had to escape from the country.

Our story begins five years after Culloden.

Where David travelled by sea and on land

Chapter 1
The house of Shaws

Early one morning in June 1751 I took the key for the last time out of the door of my father's house in Essendean. As I went down the road, the sun began to shine on the tops of the hills.

That good man Mr Campbell was waiting for me near his church.

"Have you had some breakfast, David Balfour my boy?" he asked.

"Yes, Mr Campbell. Thank you," I answered.

"Then I'll just walk with you as far as the river crossing," he said.

We walked together in silence for a time. Then Mr Campbell said, "Now, Davie, I have something to give you. After your mother died, and when that fine man your father was himself dying, he gave me a letter. He told me to give it to you when the house was sold. 'Tell him,' he said, 'to take it to the house of Shaws, not far from Cramond.' Here's the letter." And he took it out of his pocket.

"The house of Shaws!" I said. "Why did he want me to go there?"

"I don't know," said Mr Campbell. "I think your father came from there. It's a well-known house, and it's the home of a well-known family, Balfour of Shaws. Perhaps your father was of that family, though he never spoke about it. He was certainly a man of much greater learning than the ordinary village school teacher."

Mr Campbell put the letter into my hand, and I read on it: "To Ebenezer Balfour of Shaws. This letter is to be given to him by my son David Balfour."

My heart beat hard at the thought of going to a great house. I had seen myself as just the seventeen-year-old son of a poor country teacher. I had set out to go to Edinburgh; I hoped to become a student in one of the great schools there or in Holland.

"Mr Campbell," I said, "do you think I ought to go?"

"Yes," he answered. "Cramond isn't far from Edinburgh. A strong lad like you can get there in two days' walking. At the worst, they can only tell you to go away, but I think your father must have expected something else."

At the river, Mr Campbell took my hand in both his hands. He looked into my eyes, and I saw tears coming into his own eyes.

"Goodbye, Davie," he said. "May God be with you!" And he turned and hurried away, back towards Essendean. He never looked back, and I stood and watched him. I knew his hurry was to hide his sadness at my leaving Essendean, and I felt bad about wanting to get away from the quiet village.

At last I picked up the little bag that held everything that was mine. I crossed the river and started up the hill beyond it. From the top of the hill I could see the wide sheep-road that I had to follow. I looked back once more at the Essendean church and the tall trees round it, where my father and mother lay.

Two days later, I came in the morning to the top of a hill. I could see the city of Edinburgh and beyond it the sea. Although they were far away, I could see a flag on Edinburgh Castle and ships on the firth.

I started down the hill. After a time I saw a man looking after sheep. He pointed to the way I should walk to get to Cramond, to the west of the city. On my way down, I asked several more people, and at last I came to the road that leads from Edinburgh to Glasgow. Before I could cross it, I had to wait while a large body of soldiers came along the road. I was excited to see them in their red coats, moving in step to the music of their band.

When I was near to Cramond, I began to ask the way to the house of Shaws. The question seemed to surprise the people I asked. At first I thought it was because the lad who asked it was in simple country clothes, dusty from the road, not one to have business at a great house. But when I got the same look from several other people, I wondered if there was something strange about the house itself. So I changed the question for the next man I met.

3

"Have you heard of a house called the house of Shaws somewhere near here?" I asked.

"Yes," he said. "Why?"

"It's a big house, is it?" I said.

"Oh yes. It's big."

"And the people in it?"

"People?" he cried. "What's the matter with you? There aren't any people."

"Oh!" I said. "Not Mr Ebenezer?"

"Oh yes. The laird's there – if it's him you want to see. What do you want from him?"

"They told me I might get work," I said.

"What!" he said, very sharply. "Well, lad, it's not my business, but you seem a nice lad, so I'll say keep away from the Shaws. Keep away!"

At last I found the house, and I sat down and looked. The country all round the house looked good. There were sheep in the fields and flowers on the banks. But I didn't like the look of the house. Only one part of it seemed to be finished. The main part had its walls but no roof, and no glass in the windows.

The sun had gone down, and night had begun to fall as I got near to the unfinished building. I saw that in one room there was the poor light of a little fire. I went to the thick wooden door and hit it – not very bravely – with the end of my stick.

Silence.

4

No. Not the silence of an empty house. It was as if anybody in the house had stopped moving to listen. I could hear a clock when I put my ear to the door. I thought of running away, but suddenly I was angry. I hit the door and kicked it and shouted for Mr Balfour.

There was a sound right above my head. I jumped back and looked up – into the mouth of an old gun at one of the windows.

"It's loaded," said a voice.

"I've come here with a letter," I said, "to Mr Ebenezer Balfour of Shaws. Is he here?"

"Who is it from?" the man with the gun asked.

"That's not your business," I said. I was getting angry again.

"Well," he said, "you can put it down outside the door, and go away."

"Certainly not!" I said. "I'll put it into Mr Balfour's hand. It's a letter about myself."

"And who are you?" was the next question, after a minute's silence.

"My name is David Balfour."

I knew that the man with the gun was surprised by that answer. I heard the gun touch the side of the window. There was another silence, then: "Is your father dead? – Yes, he's dead, I suppose, or you wouldn't be here." More silence, and at last: "Well, wait there and I'll let you in."

Chapter 2
My uncle

After a time, there was a great noise of locks and iron bars. The door opened a little, and was quickly shut again as soon as I was in.

"Go into the kitchen, but don't touch anything," the man said. And he started locking and barring the door again.

I found the kitchen. There was no lamp, but I could see by the light of the fire that it was a big room with stone walls. There were a few pots and plates, and there was a table ready for one person's supper with a plate of porridge, a spoon, and a cup of beer. The only other things in the kitchen were big boxes standing along the wall, each with a heavy lock.

When the last bar was in place on the door, the man came into the kitchen. He was a small, unhealthy-looking man, about sixty years old. He watched me all the time but never looked me in the face. I couldn't think what he was or what work he was supposed to do.

"Are you hungry?" he asked, with his eyes fixed on my knees. "You can have that porridge."

"But it's your supper, isn't it?" I said.

"Well," he said, "I don't need it. But I'll have the beer." He drank most of it, then held out his hand, saying, "Give me the letter."

"The letter isn't for you," I said. "It's for Mr Balfour."

"And who do you think I am? Give me Alexander's letter."

"You know my father's name?"

"It would be strange if I didn't," he said. "He was my brother, and – even though you don't seem to like me or my house or my good porridge, Davie – I'm your uncle. So give me the letter, and sit down and eat. If you're thirsty, you'll find water behind the door."

I gave him the letter, then ate some of the porridge in silence.

"How long has your father been dead?" he asked suddenly.

"Three weeks, sir," I answered.

"He was a secret man – a secret, silent man. He never said much. He won't have told you much about me?"

I said, "I never knew he had a brother."

"Ah!" he said. "And perhaps he never said anything about Shaws?"

"I never even heard the name."

"Strange," he said. But he seemed pleased for some reason. "Now it's time for bed. I'll show you the way."

Without a lamp or a candle, he led me along a dark passage and up some stairs, and un-locked a door.

"There it is," he said.

The room was black dark.

David gives the letter to his uncle

"I need a light," I told him.

"No lights in this house," he said. "I'm afraid of fire. Good night." And he pushed me into the room. I heard him lock the door.

I didn't know whether to laugh or cry. The room was cold, and the bed – when I found it – was not dry. But I had picked up my bag and my plaid before I left the kitchen. I rolled myself up in the plaid and lay on the floor with my head on my bag, and I was soon asleep.

The next morning, breakfast was the same small meal of porridge and beer as the supper of the night before.

In the room next to the kitchen I found a lot of books in Latin and English. I love reading, and I looked at them with interest. Just inside the cover of one of the books I found, in my father's writing:

To my brother Ebenezer on his fifth birthday

I couldn't understand that. The writing was clearly my father's, and not childish. I had supposed that Ebenezer was the older of the two brothers. He had the house, and my father had been just a poor teacher. What did it mean?

I looked at the books and cleaned the room. It was a hot day, and by nightfall I thought there was a storm coming.

My uncle spoke very kindly to me at supper time.

"You'll help me with the house and garden, Davie lad," he said. "And I'll help you. I'll need some papers for that. They're in a box at the top of the stairs at the other end of the house. The house isn't finished, so you can only get to the stairs from the outside. Here's the key." And he pulled a big old key out of his pocket. "Go in, and up the stairs, and bring down the box."

I asked, "Can I have a lamp, sir?"

"No," he said. "No lights in this house."

He opened the big door, and I went out into the night. I found my way by touching the walls until I came to the door at the far end. The key turned the lock – not easily – and I found the stone stairs inside. I started to climb, keeping close to the wall.

I had climbed to a height of about thirty-five metres when the storm began. A sudden flash in the sky showed me the stairs for half a second. They came to an end just above the place where I was standing! There was nothing beyond the last step, just a great hole.

My uncle wanted to kill me!

I came down the stairs very carefully, feeling my way with hands and feet. Sometimes the storm lit the stairs for a second, but most of the time it was very dark, and very dangerous.

As I came out of the door, a great flash of lightning from the storm showed me my uncle at the other door. He didn't see me because the lightning flash had frightened him and he was running back into the house, leaving the door open behind him.

When I appeared in the kitchen, he was more frightened still. I wanted to ask a lot of questions but he said, "I'll tell you all about it in the morning. Let me go to bed now, Davie. I'm sick – very sick."

I locked him in his room. Then I went back to the kitchen, built up a big fire, rolled myself in my plaid, lay down on the boxes, and fell asleep.

Chapter 3
The ship

When I let my uncle out of his room, he said something about the night before being "a bit of fun". I waited for him to tell me "all about it", as he had promised. But before he could begin, we heard someone at the door.

I went to open the door and found a half-grown boy outside. He was dressed like a sailor and he looked very cold.

"I've brought a letter," he said, and he held it out, adding, "and I'm very hungry."

"Well," I said, "come into the house and I'll give you some porridge."

While the boy was eating – laughing and trying to look like a man – my uncle read the letter. Then he gave it to me and told me to read it. It said:

Sir,

I am now at the Hawes Inn at the Queen's Ferry, and my ship is ready for sea. If you have any more orders for me, let me have them today, as we have a good wind to take us out of the firth.

I have had some small quarrels with your lawyer, Mr Rankeillor, and I am afraid we may lose some money for that reason.

Yours truly,   *Elias Hoseason*

When I had read it, my uncle said, "You see, Davie, I have some business with this man Hoseason. He is the captain of a ship, the *Covenant*. Now, if you and I walked to the Queen's Ferry with this boy, I could see the captain at the Hawes Inn. I could put my name to any papers, and then we could go on to see Mr Rankeillor, the lawyer. Perhaps you won't believe me any more, but you'll believe him. He is the lawyer for half the gentlemen in this part of the country, and he knew your father."

I thought about it. It seemed safe enough to say yes, and from the Queen's Ferry I could make him go to the lawyer's, even if he didn't really want to.

So we set out. My uncle walked by himself at the side of the road and never said a word all the way. But the boy talked. He told me his name was Ransome. "I've been at sea since I was nine," he told me. He spoke of many bad things he had done, things that he thought were manly. I didn't believe all of them. I listened and said nothing.

I asked him about the ship. "There isn't a finer ship on the sea," he said. And about Captain Hoseason: "He's a fine captain. He isn't afraid of anything or anybody. He'll keep all sail on his ship in the strongest wind. He's rough and hard. I expect he's killed a few men."

The boy could see nothing wrong in the

13

man, except: "He isn't a seaman. It's Mr Shuan that knows how to take the ship anywhere in the world. He's the best seaman in the world, except for drink. A real man, Mr Shuan is! Look." The boy turned up his trousers and showed me a great, red wound – a fearful wound. "Mr Shuan did that. He's a man, he is!"

I felt very sorry for the poor weak-minded boy, but he didn't seem sorry for himself.

"There are others who really do have a bad time," Ransome told me. "There are the twenty-pounders. They really are unhappy. And there are the children too. I keep them in order, I tell you!"

He went on talking, and I came to understand his "twenty-pounders". They were the unhappy thieves and other wrongdoers who were sent by the judges to work in the plantations in North America. The government paid twenty pounds each to the ship's captain to take them there. The "children", it seemed, had been kidnapped and were to be sold – if they were still alive – when the ship arrived in America.

At the Queen's Ferry my uncle went into the Hawes Inn to see Captain Hoseason. I had promised myself not to let my uncle out of my sight, but foolishly I forgot that when he and the captain began a long talk over a great number of papers.

14

I crossed the road in front of the inn, and walked down to the water's edge. The ship's boat was there, waiting for the captain. The sailors standing near the boat looked very rough.

The innkeeper spoke to me.

"Was it you who came with Ebenezer?" he asked.

"Yes. – But I'm not a part of his family."

"No," he said. "I wouldn't think so. But there's something about you that makes me remember Mr Alexander. Now he *was* a good man."

"You mean that Ebenezer isn't good?"

The innkeeper shook his head. "He's a bad old man – a very bad old man. But he was once a fine young man too – like Mr Alexander."

While he was speaking, I saw Captain Hoseason go down to the men near the ship's boat. He spoke to them as if he was giving orders. Then he came back towards the inn, a fine tall gentleman, not like the rough hard man I had expected from Ransome's stories.

He came towards me and shook hands.

"Sir," he said, "Mr Balfour has been telling me about you. You look a fine young man. I wish I was going to be here longer to get to know you better. But you must come on board my ship with your uncle, and we'll have a drink together."

I certainly wanted to see the inside of a ship,

but I wasn't going to put myself into danger of any kind. I told the captain that my uncle and I had to see a lawyer that afternoon.

"Yes," said the captain, "he told me about that. But we'll sail very close to the town landing-place. The ship's boat will take you to it, and you'll be very near to Rankeillor's place." And then, as my uncle came towards us, the captain suddenly said very quietly in my ear: "Be careful of the old fox. He's planning something against you. Come on board the ship and I'll be able to tell you secretly about it."

He took my arm in a very friendly way and led me to the waterside. I thought (like a poor fool!) that I had found a friend and helper, and I let him help me to get into the boat beside my uncle.

When we reached the ship, the captain climbed quickly up and then called to me to follow him. When I arrived on deck, he put his arm though mine and started pointing out all the interesting things on the ship. I had never been on a ship, and the sights and the movement made me forget other things for a time.

"But where is my uncle?" I said suddenly.

"You're right to ask," said Hoseason, not friendly now.

I felt I was lost. I freed myself from his hold and ran to the side of the ship. Yes, there was the boat going towards the town, with my uncle sitting in it. I gave a loud cry – "Help! Help" – so that my uncle turned round and showed me a face in which cruelty and fear were mixed.

That was the last I saw. Strong hands were already pulling me away from the ship's side, and now there was a crash; I saw a great flash of fire, and – black darkness.

Chapter 4
To sea

I woke in darkness. My hands and my feet were tied, and I was in great pain. There were noises I had never heard before – all the noises of a ship driving through heavy seas, with the cries of seamen fighting with the sails in a high wind. My whole world rose up, shaking, and then fell – down, down, endlessly it seemed – then slowly up again. With the pain and sickness, my mind cleared very slowly. At last I understood: I was tied up, somewhere far down in a ship, and the wind had become a storm. What a fool I had been! How hateful my uncle was! What was going to happen to me? my thoughts went round and round, and – stopped! My world seemed to come to an end.

A lamp shining in my face woke me. A small man with green eyes and unbrushed fair hair was looking down at me.

"Well," he said, "how are you?"

I couldn't answer. He touched me quite gently to see how ill I was, and then he began to wash and cover the wound on my head.

"Yes," he said, "it's a bad wound. It'll hurt for quite a long time. Have you had any food?"

"I couldn't eat anthing," I said.

He gave me a drink in a tin cup, and then went away.

I was still in pain and very ill when he came again – I don't know how long after. This time the captain came with him.

"Now why have you brought me here, Mr Riach?" the captain asked.

"You can see, sir," said Riach. "He's very ill. He can't eat. There's no light and very little air. The boy must be taken out of here and put in the men's sleeping place."

"He stays here," said the captain.

"That's not the answer."

Hoseason was very angry. He was even angrier when Riach caught him by the arm and said, " I am paid to be the second officer of this old ship. I'm not paid to do anything else. Even if *you* have been paid to do a murder——"

"What!" cried Hoseason. "What kind of talk is that? You've sailed with me for a few years and you ought to know me better. I'm a hard man, but I'm not a murderer. If you say the lad will die——"

"Yes, he will."

"All right. Put him where you like."

A few minutes later, somebody untied me. I was put on a man's back and carried up to the seamen's sleeping place. There they laid me down on a narrow bed, and I knew nothing else for hours or days.

The men were kind to me in their way. Mr Riach visited me and said I would soon be well.

He sent one of the men to me with a drink.

"This'll be good for you," the man said. "You'll be all right. A bang on the head's nothing. It was me that gave it to you."

They gave me back my money – most of it – that they had taken for themselves. "You may want it," they said. The ship, they told me, was going to the Carolinas. In those days – when I was young – men were still sold for work in the plantations, white men as well as black men. That was what my cruel uncle had planned for me.

The ship's boy, Ransome, came in sometimes from the roundhouse, where he slept. He was always in pain from some cruelty of Mr Shuan's, but the men thought the first officer was a fine man – "the only real seaman on the ship, and not a bad man when the drink isn't in him".

Day after day and night after night the ship fought its way towards the north against strong winds blowing from the north. I grew better and stronger, but I was not allowed to leave the sleeping place.

One night, about twelve o'clock, one of the seamen came down for his coat. Soon the men who were not working began to say to each other, "Shuan has done it at last." There was no need to say what he had done or who he had done it to. We all knew. But we didn't expect the thing that happened next. Captain

Hoseason came into the men's sleeping place, looked round, and came to me.

He spoke quite kindly as he said to me, "We want you to serve in the roundhouse. You and Ransome are to change places. Away you go at once."

I ran up from the sleeping place – and was nearly washed over the side by a wave that came rushing over the deck. I was saved by one of the seamen who had been kind to me. He showed me how to move over the deck, holding on to one thing after another. And he pointed to the roundhouse. On my way there I passed two seamen who, with great difficulty, were carrying Ransome to the place I had left.

Chapter 5
The roundhouse

The roundhouse wasn't round. It was square. (I learnt later that it was called the "roundhouse" because you could walk round it on the deck.) It had a table and two narrow beds, one for the captain and the other for the first or second officer, whichever was not on deck. There was a store-room under the roundhouse with all the best food and drink, all the gunpowder, and all the guns except the two big guns on deck. There were one or two of the short seamen's swords they call cutlasses, but most of the cutlasses were outside.

There was one small window on each side and a glass cover to an opening – a skylight – in the roof. The two doors were very strong to stand against the power of the sea rushing along the deck.

When I arrived, Mr Shuan was sitting at the table with a bottle in front of him. Captain Hoseason came in. He said nothing but stood looking at his first officer. After a time, Mr Riach came in.

"The boy's dead," he told the captain.

Mr Shuan said nothing, but he put out his hand to take the bottle. Mr Riach was quicker and took the bottle away. Mr Shuan jumped up.

He wanted to kill the second officer, but the captain stopped him.

"Sit down!" Hoseason shouted. "You drunken fool! Do you know what you've done? You've murdered the boy!"

Shuan seemed to understand. He sat down and put his head in his hands.

"Well," he said, "he brought me a dirty cup."

Hoseason took him by the arm, led him to his bed, and told him to lie down and go to sleep. He spoke as a father might speak to a bad child. The murderer cried a little, but he lay down.

I quickly learnt what I had to do in the roundhouse. I had to serve the meals. The captain ate at fixed times with the officer who was not on deck. All through the day I had to be ready to take a drink to one or more of the three officers. They drank endlessly. I don't know how they kept healthy. My bed was my plaid on the floor of the roundhouse, but I never slept for long before an officer came in from the deck wanting a drink.

For ten more days the *Covenant* fought her way north and then west against strong winds. At last the captain turned south to try to find a way round the south of Ireland.

After a time we seemed to have less wind, but there was heavy rain and it was hard to see anything. At about ten at night, I was serving supper to Mr Riach and the captain when the ship struck something. The two men jumped up.

"Rocks," cried Mr Riach.

"No," said Hoseason. "We've hit a boat."

The captain was right. We had hit a boat in the darkness. It had broken in two, and all the men in it had gone down with it except for one man. This one man had jumped up and caught hold of a part of the ship.

Hoseason brought him into the roundhouse. He was a smallish man, but strong-looking. By his smile you wouldn't have thought he had just had a wonderful escape. His face was dark from the sun, and his eyes were unusually light, with a kind of dancing fearlessness in them. When he took off his cloak, he put two very fine silver-covered pistols on the table, and I saw that he had a long sword at his side.

The captain was looking at him too, but at the clothes more than at the man. They were certainly very fine clothes for the roundhouse of a ship like the *Covenant*, though they showed that the wearer had had a rough time.

"A fine French coat," Hoseason said.

"Oho!" said the stranger. "You mean——" And he put his hands quickly on his pistols.

"Not so quick," said the captain. "Don't be in a hurry to do something that may not be necessary."

The stranger on the ship

"Oh," said the gentleman. "Are you one of us?"

"A Jacobite? No. But I can be sorry to see another man in trouble for what he believes."

"Can you really?" asked the Jacobite. "Well, sir, yes, to tell the truth, I am one of those who were in trouble about the years 1745–46. And to be quite plain, if I got into the hands of the redcoats, it would still be very bad. Now, sir, I was going to France. There was a French ship somewhere near here to take me to France, but we missed each other in the darkness and the rain. I have some money. It isn't mine: it's my chieftain's. But I can use a little to get the rest of it to him. Will you take me to France, captain?"

"No," said Hoseason. "I can't do that. But I might put you on land near here. I'd like to see the money first, of course."

He saw me in the corner and sent me away to get supper for the Jacobite. I was very quick, and when I came back I saw the stranger paying sixty pounds out of a heavy money bag. He and the captain shook hands, and I heard Hoseason say, "That's my promise, then. I'll take you to the Linnhe Loch and land you safely there for your sixty pounds. I'll just go and give the necessary orders." And he left the roundhouse.

I had heard about the people of the Highlands who paid twice for the use of their land: once to the government or the new laird, and once to their old chieftains. Many of the Highlanders' chieftains were living in France, and I knew, too, about the brave men who took the money from the clans to the chieftains although they would be put to death if they were caught. Here, then, was one of those brave men.

"So you're a Jacobite, are you?" I said, as I put the porridge in front of him.

"Yes," he said, beginning to eat. "And your long face tells me you're a Whig."

"More or less," I said, though I was as good a Whig as Mr Campbell could make me.

"Well, Mr More-or-less, this bottle's empty. If I'm paying sixty pounds, I think I ought to have another bottle."

I went out to get the key of the store from the captain, and I saw him and the two officers with their heads close together. I heard Mr Riach say, "Can't we get him to leave the roundhouse for some reason?"

"He's better where he is," answered Hoseason. "He can't use his sword in there."

My first thought was to turn away from these murderous men. But I changed my mind. "Captain," I said, "the gentleman wants a drink. Please may I have the key?"

They all turned round.

"Here's our chance to get the guns," said Riach. And then to me: "Do you know where the pistols are, David?"

"Yes, yes," said Hoseason, "David knows.

27

David's a good lad. You see, David, that High-lander is a danger to the ship and an enemy of King George. You'll help us, won't you, David?"

I had never been so "David"ed since I came on board. They promised to give me some of the gold from the Jacobite's bag if I would help them. Then they told me what to do and sent me back with the keys to the drinks and gun stores.

The Jacobite was eating his supper when I went into the roundhouse. I put my hand on his arm and said, "Do you want to be killed?"

He stood up quickly. "What do you mean?" he asked.

"They're all murderers on this ship," I said. "They've murdered a boy already. Now it's you."

"Ah!" he said. "But they haven't got me yet. Will you help me?"

"I will," I said. "I'm not a thief or a mur-derer. I'll help you."

"Good," he said. "What's your name?"

"David Balfour," I said. And because I thought he must like important names, I added: "David Balfour of Shaws."

"My name is Stewart," he said. "They call me Alan Breck, but Stewart – a king's name – is good enough for me, although I don't have any 'of' to add."

Then we looked at the roundhouse. I shut

one of the strong doors, and I was going to shut the other when he stopped me.

"No, David," he said. "While the door is open and my face is towards it, most of my enemies will be in front of me – which is where I like my enemies to be."

Then he asked me to sit at the table with gunpowder and bullets and to load all the pistols. "And listen to me while you are doing that," he said. "How many are against us?"

"Fifteen," I said.

"Oh!" Alan said, and was silent for a minute. Then: "I'll be at this door. If they try to break in at the other door, that's part of your work. When you've loaded the pistols, stand on that bed beside the window. Then if they go to the other door, you can shoot."

I'm not brave. My mouth was dry when I thought of the numbers against us. But I did what he asked me to do.

Chapter 6
We hold the roundhouse

The men on deck waited for me to go back to them, but at last the captain came to the open door.

"Stop!" said Alan, and pointed his sword at him.

The captain said nothing, but he turned towards me with a very ugly look before he want away. Soon after that, I heard them giving out the cutlasses.

It came suddenly. There was a rush and a shout. I heard a cry as if someone was hurt, and I looked across. One man was on the deck, wounded. Mr Shuan was at the door, attacking Alan.

"That's the man that killed the boy," I called.

"You watch your window!" said Alan, and as I turned back I saw his sword point go through the first officer's body.

I looked quickly through my window, just in time to see five men running towards the closed door with a heavy length of wood. I shot at them with my first pistol, and I heard one of them cry out as the bullet hit him. I had never used a pistol before. The bullet from my next pistol went over their heads, and the third didn't seem to hurt anybody. But they threw down the length of wood and ran away.

The roundhouse was full of smoke from my pistols, and it was hard to see across from one side to the other. There was blood on Alan's sword, and he looked very pleased with himself. Mr Shuan was on the floor, and men were pulling him out by his feet.

"They'll be back, David," Alan said. "Watch from your window."

I loaded the three pistols I had used. Then I waited.

Suddenly a group of men with cutlasses rushed to the open door. At the same time the glass of the skylight in the roof was broken into a thousand pieces and a man dropped through. His cutlass fell from his hand, and before he could pick it up, I put a pistol to his back.

But I found I couldn't shoot a moving, living man. He turned quickly, with a shout, and took hold of me. Then – perhaps because that made me brave, or perhaps because I was so frightened – I cried out and shot him in the middle of his body. With an ugly sound – Aargh! – he fell to the floor.

Just then the leg of a second man, who was following him through the skylight, hit me on the head. I quickly picked up another pistol and shot this man in the leg.

"David!" Alan's voice made me move away from the two bodies on the floor. While he was fighting others, one seaman had run in under his sword, and had taken hold of his body.

Another had got in and had his cutlass up. The roof stopped it, but the danger was still there. I picked up the cutlass of one of the men on the floor and sprang to help Alan. It wasn't necessary. Before I could do anything, Alan had jumped back to give himself space, and had then attacked, shouting and using his sword like lightning. They turned to escape, falling over each other in their hurry. The sword in Alan's hand flashed again and again, and at each flash there was the cry of a wounded man. He drove them out and along the deck like a sheepdog driving sheep. They were still running and crying out in fear after he had turned and come back to the roundhouse.

There were four of the men, dead or seriously wounded, inside the roundhouse. Alan and I threw them out. Then he turned to me.

"David," he cried, "come to my arms. I love you like a brother. And oh, man, am I not a bonny fighter?"

Nothing else happened for a long time. One of us sat at the door and watched while the other slept. At about six o'clock in the morning we sat down to breakfast. Alan ate quite a lot, but I had been in my first fight, and had seen men killed and wounded for the first time, so I couldn't eat much.

Alan made up a song in the Gaelic about Alan Breck and his sword. He told me what it meant. It didn't say much about my part in the fight, but poets have to think about the sounds of their poetry. In ordinary talk, Alan was always more than fair to me, even though he was almost childishly pleased with himself.

He cut off one of the silver buttons from his coat.

"My father, Duncan Stewart, gave me these silver buttons," he said. "Now I'm giving one to you. Keep it to remember last night's work. And wherever you go, and show the button, the friends of Alan Breck will stand with you."

He said it as if he were Charlemagne and had armies to obey him. Although he was the bravest man I have ever known, I often wanted to smile at his love of himself.

Mr Riach called from the deck. The captain wanted to talk to Alan.

"And how do we know what he will try to do?" I said.

"He won't try anything," Riach answered. "Even if he wanted to, the men wouldn't help him."

"Oh?"

"It's true," he said. "And it's not only the men. It's me as well. I've had enough, and I'm frightened, Davie. What we want is to see the Jacobite leave the ship. We'll take him to the Linnhe Loch."

Chapter 7
I hear about the "Red Fox"

From where the ship was, the nearest way to the Linnhe Loch was through a narrow seaway to the north of the island of Mull. But the captain didn't know that way, so we sailed all day along the west of Mull to come round the south of the island.

Alan and I made an exchange with the captain. We exchanged a bottle of the captain's drink for enough water to wash the blood from the roundhouse floor. Then he and I sat in the roundhouse with the doors open. That was when we heard each other's stories.

First I told him everything that had happened to me. He listened kindly except when I spoke about that good friend of mine in Essendean, Mr Campbell. At that point he cried out that he hated everybody with that name.

"Why?" I asked. "Mr Campbell is a man I would give my life for."

"And I," said Alan, "would give nothing to any Campbell except a bullet."

"Why?" I asked again. "What's wrong with the Campbells?"

"Well," he said, "you know I'm a Stewart from Appin. The Campbells have always been our enemies. They have tried everything – except the sword, never the sword – to get our lands and our houses. They have used lies – lying words, lying papers, lying lawyers – but never the sword. It's the Campbells that make life so dangerous for men like myself."

"And yet you come back?"

"Oh yes!" said Alan. "I have been back every year since forty-six. You see, I have to see my friends and my country. France is a fine place, of course, but I have to see the heather and the deer. And then there's the business of my chieftain, Ardshiel."

"Business?" I said.

"You see, David. He was all his life a great man, with a king's name, and four hundred swordsmen to come at his call. And now he has to live in a French town like a poor person. His children, the hope of Appin, must be taught so that they can lead their people. Now, the people of Appin have to pay King George for the use of their land, but they are true to their chief, and the poor people find a second payment for Ardshiel. Well, David, I'm the person that carries it." And he struck the money bag hard with his hand. "Ardshiel's brother, James Stewart, sometimes called James of the Glens, gets it in, and I carry it."

I heard him, but my mind was on the clansmen's love of their chieftain.

"I call it fine, the way they look after their chief," I said. "I'm a Whig, more or less, but I call it fine."

"Yes," he said. "You're a Whig, but you're a gentleman and that's why you understand it. But if you were one of the Campbells, you would hate to hear about it. If you were the Red Fox——" He stopped. The look in his eyes showed how he hated the name.

"The Red Fox?" I said. "Who is he?

"I'll tell you," cried Alan. "When the men of the clans were broken at Culloden, and the horses rode through the best blood of the north, Ardshiel had to run like a poor deer on the mountains – he and his lady and their children. We had hard work before we could get them to France. While he was still hidden in the heather, the English beasts, who couldn't take his life, were striking at his rights. They took away all his power; they took his land; they took the swords and guns from his clansmen. They made laws against wearing tartan; a man can be sent to prison for wearing a kilt. One thing they could not kill: the love the clansmen have for their chief."

"The money you carry shows that," I said.

"Yes. But now we come to a man, a Campbell, red-haired Colin of Glenure——'

"The man you call the Red Fox?" I said.

"Yes. He got papers from King George that made him the king's controller for the lands of Appin. When he learnt that the clansmen were paying for their land not only to him but also to Ardshiel, he was very angry. He sent for lawyers and papers and redcoats, and he had all Ardshiel's people driven out of their homes and their lands. The soldiers are still there, hundreds of them, but the money still gets through to Ardshiel."

"There's one thing I don't understand," I said. "The Highlands are covered with redcoats. How does a man like you come and go without being caught?"

"It's easier than you would think," said Alan. "An open hillside is like one wide road. If there's a soldier at one place, you just go another way. Heather's a wonderful help. And everywhere you find friends to tell you where the redcoats are, and friends with houses and farms where you can hide. Besides, the soldiers don't watch so well, because the Highlands have been "pacified". By that they mean that the country has been made peaceful, without a gun or a sword in the hands of the clansmen – though there may be a few hidden in roofs and other places."

Chapter 8
We strike rocks

As we drew nearer to the island of Mull, there were more and more rocks in the sea. The sea itself began to run more quickly. The captain had sent a look-out man high up, and this man suddenly called: "Rocks! Keep out from the land!"

There were two men at the wheel, and they threw their weight on it. But just then the wind changed, and the ship was turned by the movement of the sea – right on to the rocks! There was a crash, and we were thrown off our feet.

Mr Riach and the few seamen who could do it began to get the ship's boat ready. The men had left all kinds of things in the boat, which was on deck in the middle of the ship. I ran to help.

Suddenly a voice cried, "Hold on!"

A huge wave threw the ship right over on one side. I looked for something to hold on to, but I was too late. The movement of the ship and the sea that came over the deck sent me over the side of the ship.

I went down in the water, fought my way up, was pushed under by another wave. I don't know how many times I went down while the rough water rushed me away from the ship.

After a time I found I was holding on to a

piece of wood from the ship, and then suddenly I was in quieter water. I looked for the ship, and I was surprised to see how far the sea had taken me. I could still see the ship, but I couldn't see whether they had yet got the boat into the water.

I saw land not very far away. I am not a good swimmer, but I held on to the piece of wood and kicked with my legs. After about an hour I could put my feet on the bottom and walk to the land.

I was wet, very tired, cold and hungry. I started to walk away from the sea, hoping to find a house. "In a house," I thought," I can get dry and warm, and they can tell me about the ship and the men on it."

It was rough ground to walk over: nothing but rocks with heather among them. I walked until I came to water. There was land beyond the water, but I couldn't reach it. I turned and followed the water's edge, climbing and falling over the rocks. After a time, I saw that the land beyond the water was farther away. I turned again and tried to find a crossing the other way. No. I was on a small island with no houses and no people. The big island of Mull was across the water.

In the end, I crossed the small island again and looked for my piece of wood. Carrying it across the island nearly killed me, but I got it into the water at the nearest point to Mull. After

David in the water

a rest, I swam across with it. As I climbed up the rocks on the other side, a piece of money fell from my pocket. When the sailors gave me back my money, they kept some, and they also kept my father's money bag, so my money was in my pocket without a bag. Now I found that climbing and swimming had made a hole in my pocket. Most of my money had gone to the bottom of the sea. I had left Essendean with more than fifty pounds. Now I had just over three pounds.

Chapter 9
The lad with the silver button

That part of Mull was like the small island, all rocks and heather and nothing else. I was so tired and wet and weak that I found a place between two rocks and lay down.

I suppose I slept, although I was so cold. The sun woke me, and I found a very small stream with clear water that I could drink. I went to sleep again in the sun beside the stream. It was afternoon when I climbed a hill and looked at the country from the top.

There was smoke to the north-east – smoke that meant a house – and I started walking towards it. I was still very tired, and the walk, through and over rocks and heather, took several hours.

I reached the house at about six o'clock in the evening. It was long and low, built of stone, and with what looked like grass growing on the roof. I saw a lot of houses like that in the Highlands. An old man was sitting outside in the evening sun. He didn't speak English easily, but I understood that men from the ship had landed safely and had had a meal at his house the day before.

"Was there one," I asked, "dressed like a gentleman?"

He told me that one of them, who had come

alone, was a gentleman, a Highland gentleman.

"Ah!" I said, "and he had a feather in his hat?"

He said that the gentleman had no hat.

At first I thought Alan had lost his hat, but then I remembered the rain. I supposed that he was keeping it under his coat. I smiled.

"Oh!" cried the old man. "You're the lad with the silver button!"

"Yes." And I showed it to him, glad that it hadn't been in the pocket with the hole.

"Well, then, your friend says you must follow him to his country by way of Torosay." And he led me into his little house as if it had been a palace.

His wife could speak no English at all, but she smiled and put in front of me the best food they had, while the old man made a wonderful drink of whisky and other things. After that, I slept well. It was nearly twelve o'clock when I woke up next day and ate the breakfast the old woman prepared for me.

I tried to pay something – I could see they were very poor – but they wouldn't take anything. The old man came to the door with me.

"That's the way to Torosay," he said. "There are no roads. You'll have to ask."

I did ask. There were plenty of people about, working hard to get a living out of very small fields of poor earth, or looking after a few thin cows. Their clothes were strange. There were new laws against wearing their Highland dress because the tartan showed a man's clan, and the government wanted to break up the clans. On the mainland, the Highlanders had to wear the dress of Lowlanders, which they hated. But here on the island of Mull, although it wasn't safe to wear tartan or the kilt, at least there was nobody to make them wear the clothes they hated.

Very few of them could speak English. When I was lost, I said, "Torosay?" and pointed. I expected them to point. But out of their mouths came a stream of the Gaelic, which I couldn't understand. The result was that I got lost again and again. My journey took me a long time.

There is a boat every day from Torosay to Kinlochaline on the mainland. Both Torosay and Kinlochaline are in the country of the Maclean clan, but the boat was sailed by a man called Neil Roy Macrob, and I knew that Macrob was one of the names of Alan's clansmen. So I wanted to talk to Neil Roy. I couldn't do it while the boat was full of people.

At Kinlochaline, Neil Roy was alone for a time, and I went to him.

"You're one of the Appin men, aren't you?" I said.

"Why not?" he answered.

I said, "I'm looking for somebody, and I think

you may know where he is. His name is Alan Breck Stewart."

He became very unfriendly. "The man you ask for is in France," he said.

I saw that I had made a mistake. I didn't say I was sorry; I just showed him the button.

"Well," he said, "you ought to have shown me that first. But if you're the lad with the silver button, I have to help you on your way. You must stay in Kinlochaline tonight. Then tomorrow you can cross Morven to Corran on the Linnhe Loch. You'll find my brother Alec there, and he'll take you on in his boat."

I thanked him and said the names again, just to be sure.

"That's right," he said. "And listen to me: there is a name you must never say, and that is the name of Alan Breck. And don't speak to anyone on the way; keep away from Whigs, Campbells and the red soldiers. If you see any redcoats, leave the road and lie in a bush."

Chapter 10
The "Red Fox" dies

Neil Roy Macrob's brother took me in his boat to a place in Alan's country of Appin. The place where I landed was just below a small forest, the wood of Lettermore. Beyond the wood, and everywhere else that I could see, there were high mountains, rough and treeless.

There was a narrow road where I landed, and I sat down beside it and looked round. After a time, I heard men and horses on the road. Three travellers came in sight. The first was a great, red-headed man, very important-looking and very hot and red in the face. The second was in black clothes, certainly a lawyer. The third was a servant; some of his clothes were in tartan. I didn't know then, but the tartan was that of the Campbells. I did know that it was against the new laws to wear tartan, and so I supposed the first man was important enough to be able to break the law.

The men stopped when they saw me.

"What are you doing here?" the red-headed man asked.

"I'm on my way to find James of the Glens in Aucharn," I said.

"James of the Glens?" He turned to the lawyer. "Is he gathering his people, do you think?"

"Well, Glenure," said the lawyer, "whether he is or not, we ought – as I told you before – to wait here for the soldiers."

I knew then that the red-haired man was Colin of Glenure, the "Red Fox".

"You needn't be afraid of me," I said. "I'm not one of James Stewart's men, and I'm not one of yours. I'm nobody's man except King George's."

"Well said, young man. But I must tell you that I have power here."

As he spoke, a shot rang out from somewhere up the hillside. At the same time, Glenure fell down on the road.

"I'm dead!" he said. "Take care of yourselves. I'm dead."

The lawyer went down on his knees and took Glenure in his arms, but there was nothing he could do.

For a second I did nothing. Then I cried out, "The murderer!" and started to run through the trees and up the hill beyond.

As I came to the top of the first climb, I saw the murderer. He was a big man in a black coat with metal buttons, carrying a long gun.

"Here!" I shouted down to the men on the road. "I see him!"

The murderer looked back, then ran on through another group of trees and out on the open mountain above them. I followed as

The "Red Fox" is killed

quickly as I could, and I was near the higher group of trees when a voice cried, "Stop!"

I looked back. The lawyer was still on the road, shouting to me to come back. Red-coated soldiers were beginning to appear above the lower wood, carrying their guns, climbing as fast as they could.

"Come back, boy!" shouted the lawyer.

"No!" I called down to him. "You come up! He isn't far away yet."

"Ten pounds if you take that lad!" the lawyer called to the redcoats. "He's one of them! They sent him to stop Glenure and keep him talking. Get him – dead or alive!"

He was shouting to the soldiers, but I heard him clearly. I suddenly understood. They thought I was working with the murderer! That struck me like lightning, and I couldn't move.

Some of the soldiers began to move up towards me, while others put up their guns to shoot at me. Still I couldn't move.

"Quick! – In here among the trees," said a voice quite near me.

I didn't know what I was doing, but I obeyed. As I ran into the wood, I heard the guns, and the bullets flew through the trees.

Just inside the wood, I found Alan Breck, standing with a fishing-rod. He said nothing except "Come!" and started running along the side of the mountain towards Balachulish. Like a sheep I followed.

We ran through trees, round rocks on the mountain side. We went on hands and knees through the heather. We travelled so fast that my heart seemed ready to break out of my body. I couldn't think and I couldn't speak. Only I remember seeing that from time to time Alan stood up and looked back. It was clear that he wanted the soldiers to see him. Every time he did it, we heard excited shouting from the redcoats far away behind us.

After a quarter of an hour, Alan stopped, lay down in the heather, and turned to me.

"Now," he said, "this is serious. Do exactly what I do – for your life!"

Just as fast, but now much more carefully, we went back along the mountain side, a little higher up – back to where we started. And at last Alan threw himself down in the higher wood of Lettermore, where I had seen him first. He was breathing hard. I fell down beside him like a dead man.

Chapter 11
James of the Glens

Alan got up first. He went to the edge of the wood and looked out.

"The redcoats are still going away," he said when he came back to me.

"Alan," I said, "we must separate."

"Why?"

"You know very well that that Campbell man lies dead in the road, and I don't want to be part of any murder."

"Murder!" cried Alan. "Listen, Mr Balfour of Shaws. If I wanted to kill a gentleman, I wouldn't do it in my own country, to cause trouble to my clan. And I wouldn't go without a sword or a gun, and with a fishing-rod in my hand. I had no part in the killing."

I was very glad.

"But," he said, "they'll be looking for both of us for the murder, and you'll need me because you don't know the country, or how to escape."

"I don't need to escape," I said. "I have no fear of the law. The judges in Scotland are fair. I'll get justice."

"You're in the Highlands," he said. "The man that was shot was a Campbell. So your 'justice' will be in Inveraray, the Campbells' town. There will be fifteen Campbells in the jury, and the judge will be the Duke of Argyll, the biggest Campbell of them all."

"The Duke of Argyll! But he's the chief judge for Scotland!"

"Yes," said Alan, "and he's also the chieftain of his clan. And what would the clan think if a Campbell was shot and nobody was hanged? I've often noticed that you Lowlanders don't seem to be clear about right and wrong."

I had to laugh at that and, to my surprise, Alan laughed too. "But it's true," he said. "We're in the Highlands, and we'll have to run. It's hard to run and hide in the heather without shelter from sun, rain and wind. But it's harder to lie waiting for death in a redcoat prison."

We walked, and sometimes went on hands and knees, over rough mountain sides for many hours. It was very dark when we saw a light.

"That's the house of James of the Glens," said Alan. "If we can see a light at this time of night, it's because there's trouble."

He was right. James Stewart had already heard about the murder, and he knew that the redcoats were coming. Men and women were hurrying about. They were carrying guns and swords away from their usual hiding places in the house and its roof, and they were putting them in deep holes in the fields.

James's wife was looking at a large number of papers, and burning some of them.

James of the Glens

"It's not safe for you here," James said to Alan. "You can leave Ardshiel's money, and my son will take it tonight, but you two must go away at once, and get into the heather and move far away."

One of James's sons gave me some clothes and some good Highland shoes. He gave me a sword, pistols, gunpowder and bullets. Between us, Alan and I carried a bag of oats to make porridge, and a cooking pot. We had a hurried meal, and then James Stewart said:

"Now you must go. Daylight comes soon in this month of July, and tomorrow the dragoons will come riding, and the redcoats will come running. We'll have every kind of trouble, and you must be far away."

Sometimes we walked; sometimes we ran. As the night grew less dark, we walked less and ran more. But the day began when we were still a long way from any shelter. The first light showed us that we were in a great open valley between mountains. It was hard to see any cover or any shelter.

"That rock!" said Alan, pointing to a big rock about a kilometre away. "We'll have to run."

We ran, as near to the ground as we could bend. When we reached the rock I was so tired that I was nearly dropping. I have called it "a rock", but it was really two big rocks that came together at the top.

"Help me up," said Alan. And at the third try we got him on top of the rocks. Then he let his coat down and pulled me up.

It seemed a good place to hide. The tops of the two rocks made a kind of cup – not deep, but big enough to hide us from anybody on the ground.

"I've been a fool," said Alan suddenly. "First I take a wrong road, so the day has caught us in a place where we ought never to have been. And worse, we're going to be here for a long summer day without a water-bottle."

Chapter 12
In the heather

At about nine in the morning, I woke up. Alan had his hand over my mouth. "Hush!" he said very quietly. "You were talking in your sleep."

"Oh?" I said. "But why did you wake me?"

He looked over the edge of the rock with one eye and showed me that I should do the same. It was a clear day, cloudless and already very hot. A river ran through the valley, and about half a kilometre up it there were a lot of redcoats round a cooking fire. Not far from them, on the top of a rock about as high as ours, there was a look-out man, with the sun shining on his gun. All the way down the side of the river there were other soldiers. Higher up the valley we could see dragoons riding their horses up and down the river side.

Alan said, very quietly, "They began to come into the valley about two hours ago. They seem to be watching the river crossings. While they stay down near the river, we're safe up here, but if they get higher up this side of the valley, they'll be able to see us. There are fewer of them down where the river gets wider, so when night comes we'll try to get past them there."

"And what are we to do till night?" I asked.

"We lie here," he said, "and get cooked by the sun."

The soldiers in the valley

We lay there. The rock got hotter and hotter, and the sun grew more cruel.

At last, about two, we couldn't bear any more. The sun had moved so that the rock threw a little shadow on the side away from the soldiers.

"Well," said Alan, "if we're going to die, there's not much difference between the sun and a gun." And he dropped down to the ground. I followed him, and we lay in the shadow, very weak and very thirsty, for an hour or two. If a soldier had come to the rock, he would have seen us. But they all passed on the other side.

In the shadow, we grew a little stronger. So we began to move, very carefully, from rock to rock along the side of the hill. I followed Alan, and sometimes we went on our stomachs, sometimes we had to make a frightened run.

As the sun was going down, we came to a deep, fast stream running down to join the river. It was wonderful. We drank, and we put our heads under the cold water. We stayed there, hidden by the banks of the stream, waiting for night. We even mixed some cold porridge. When night came, we moved on, very carefully at first, then faster and faster as we left the valley and the soldiers behind.

For three days, we travelled by night, and by day we slept in the best shelter we could find.

We spoke only to one man, who was known to Alan. He showed us a piece of paper that offered money for the murderer of Colin of Glenure. It named Alan Breck as the murderer, "wearing a hat with a feather; a French coat, blue with silver buttons ..." His "helper" wasn't named on the paper (because nobody knew my name) but he was "a tall strong lad of about eighteen, wearing an old blue coat ..." (and the clothes and shoes I was wearing before I got others from James's son); "speaks like a Lowlander, and has no beard".

We crossed two lines of mountains. On the fourth day, as the sun rose, we saw a great open space. Most of it was red with heather, but we could see that there was a lot of wet ground. We had travelled all night, and we were very tired, but there was no one in sight, and we thought it was safe to go on. By about twelve, we were near to the middle of the open space. We stopped and lay down in a thick bush of heather to sleep.

"You sleep first," said Alan.

When he woke me, I still felt very tired, but I knew he had to have a sleep himself. I began to watch. Perhaps it was the smell of the heather under the hot sun that made me fall asleep.

I woke and looked around. Dragoons! My heart nearly stopped. They were coming towards us from the south-east, spread out, and riding their horses through the thickest parts of the heather. I shook Alan. He looked at the dragoons, and then at me. He knew I had been asleep, but he said nothing about that.

"Do you see that mountain?" he said. "It's Ben Alder, full of good hiding places. Come on."

He began to move towards the mountain on his hands and knees, very quickly, keeping in the lowest parts of the open space. There is nothing that tires you more than running on hands and knees. We did it for hour after hour. As night began to fall, we saw the dragoons gathering together.

"I'm nearly dead," I said. "Can't we stop?"

"No," said Alan. "Before day comes, you and I must be in a safe place on Ben Alder."

Chapter 13
The lawyer

Those were not the last soldiers we saw, but they were the last that came dangerously near to us until we reached the River Forth at Stirling. There were plenty of soldiers there, and we couldn't use the bridge over the river.

"We'll have to cross the firth," said Alan. "And that means a boat. If we steal one, they'll look for the thieves. Then we'll be in danger again." We walked through a village, and Alan said, "Did you notice that bonny lass outside the place that sells bread?"

"Yes," I said, "a very bonny lass."

"Right," he said. "You look bad enough – tired and with your clothes in pieces. You've got to be ill too." And he told me his plan.

We went into the little shop. Alan was almost carrying me. He put me in a chair and gave me drops of water and very small pieces of bread, while he told the girl how ill I was.

"I must get him across the firth to the Queen's Ferry to the doctor," Alan told her. And then, very quietly and close to her ear, "He has been in the heather – *you* know. The brave, brave lad!"

In the end, she took us across the firth herself in her father's boat – without telling her father.

I was in the long street of the Queen's Ferry early. I wanted to find Mr Rankeillor, the lawyer, but I was afraid I would be sent away from his door because I looked so poor.

I stood outside a fine-looking house and wondered what to do. Alan was in a wood outside the town.

A gentleman came out of the house. He looked at me and asked me what I was doing.

"I'm looking for Mr Rankeillor," I said. "I have some business with him."

"I am the man you want," he said, "but I don't know your name, or even your face."

"My name is David Balfour," I said.

I saw the surprise on his face, as he said, "Where have you come from, Mr Balfour?"

"I have come from a great many strange places, sir. But I think it would be better if I didn't tell you about it in the street."

"Yes. You're right, I suppose."

We went into the house, into a dusty room full of books and papers, and Mr Rankeillor asked me a lot of questions. Where was I born? Who was my father? My mother? Did I have any uncles? . . .

After a time, he took a notebook out of a cupboard and looked at it while he asked me more questions. Did I ever meet a man called Hoseason?

I told him how I was kidnapped, how the ship went on the rocks . . .

"Where?" he asked.

"Off the south end of the island of Mull."

"Yes," Mr Rankeillor said. "But the ship was lost" (he looked down at his notebook) "on June the twenty-seventh, and we are now in August. Your friends have been very unhappy. What can you tell me about it?"

"I could tell you all about it. But I must be sure I am talking to a friend."

He smiled. "You are thinking that I was your uncle's lawyer and man of business. 'Was' is the word. Your friend Mr Campbell has been here, and as a result I have learnt very many things about Mr Ebenezer Balfour. I do not work for him now."

"Sir," I said, "if I tell you my story, I must put a friend's life into your hands."

"It will be safe. But we will call your friend 'Mr Thomson', please, if by chance he is a Highlander. I'm afraid I can't remember Highland names."

I told him my story.

At the end of it, he said, "You have certainly been to a few places and done a few things. Your friend Mr Thomson seems to be a very interesting man, though perhaps rather bloody-minded. Our lives would be simpler if we could help him to leave us – to go, let's say, to Holland. Now I must think. While I am thinking, you can use water and soap, and I'll find some clothes that my son has left in the house."

He gave me lunch – a wonderful meal after the rough food I had had, when I had any at all. And during the meal he told me the story of my father and my uncle.

"Ebenezer was the younger brother. When he was a lad, he was good-looking. He was spoilt by his father and mother, and by his brother, your father. When the two lads fell in love with the same lovely lady, Ebenezer was sure she would want to marry him.

"Your mother, David, was a wise lass, and she didn't want the spoilt one. She told Ebenzer to go away. I told you he was the spoilt one. Well, he was just like a spoilt child. He made fearful trouble for everyone. As a result, both your grandfather and your grandmother died; he broke their hearts. Now, your father was a kind gentleman, but he was weak. The end of it was that the lady and your father went away, leaving Shaws in the hands of the unpleasant younger brother."

Chapter 14
Shaws is mine

"The best way to deal with your uncle," said Rankeillor, "is to make him say that he ordered Hoseason to kidnap you. Then we needn't take him in front of a judge to get from him Shaws and the other things that are really yours. And in that way we can keep Mr Thomson out of it."

We took the clerk who worked for Rankeillor in his office, and we went to Shaws. On the way, I went into the wood and told Alan our plan. He laughed and came with me.

"Mr Thomson," said Rankeillor, "I am pleased to meet you. But I have forgotten my glasses, so I won't know you if we meet again. Perhaps we won't meet again, because I know a ship's captain who will take you to Holland tomorrow."

Mr Rankeillor and his clerk and I stood at the corner of the house while Alan went to the door. Ebenezer treated Alan in the same way as he had treated me when I first came to Shaws. Alan was not afraid of the old man's gun.

"I've come to see you," he shouted, "about David Balfour."

"Be quiet!" said Ebenezer. "Don't shout."

Alan stopped shouting, but he said, loudly and clearly, "David Balfour. We've got him. Now, as I understand it, there are two possible answers. One: you like the lad, and you'll pay to get him back. Two: you don't want him, and you'll pay us to keep him from you."

"How much?" asked my uncle.

"Well, how much did you pay Hoseason?"

"What do you mean?" cried Ebenezer. "How do you know about Hoseason?"

"Hoseason and I are together in this. But I don't know whether he's telling me the truth or lying. It's worth a hundred pounds to you if nobody sees the lad again, he says."

"Oh, he's lying!" said Ebenezer. "I only gave him twenty pounds. Not a penny more. It's true he would get more from selling the lad in the Carolinas, but not a penny more from my pocket. No. I'm a poor man. Not more than twenty pounds."

"Thank you, Mr Balfour," said Rankeillor, stepping forward. "That's what we wanted to know. Now, I have brought some papers, and we must ask you to sign your name to them. My clerk will sign them too, because he heard what you said." The clerk stepped forward. "And Mr David Balfour is here too."

I came out from my place round the corner of the house.

We had to help the old man to stand up and to walk with us into – into Shaws – into my house.

Questions

Questions on each chapter

1 *The house of Shaws*
    1 Why did David leave Essendean? (Because . . .)
    2 Who walked with him to the river?
    3 Who was the letter addressed to?
    4 "It's loaded." What was loaded?
    5 What answer surprised the man at the window?

2 *My uncle*
    1 What was the name of David's father?
    2 What did David have for supper?
    3 Why did David sleep on the floor? (Because . . .)
    4 What did he see in the first flash of lightning?

3 *The ship*
    1 Who was Elias Hoseason?
    2 Who was Rankeillor?
    3 Who made the wound on Ransome's leg?
    4 Where was David when Ebenezer went back to the town?

4 *To sea*
    1 Who looked after David's wound?
    2 Where did the seaman carry David?
    3 Where was the ship taking David to?
    4 Where did the captain send David?

5 *The roundhouse*
    1 What was in the store-room under the roundhouse?
    2 Why was Ransome dead?
    3 What did the *Covenant* hit?
    4 How much did the stranger pay to Hoseason?
    5 What did David go to get from the captain?

6 *We hold the roundhouse*
  1 What happened to Mr Shuan?
  2 Why did the five men run away from the closed door?
  3 What happened to the men who came through the skylight?
  4 What was Alan Breck's song about?

7 *I hear about the "Red Fox"*
  1 What did Alan and David want water for?
  2 Who was Alan's chieftain?
  3 What was the real name of the "Red Fox"?
  4 What did the Red Fox do to Ardshiel's people?

8 *We strike rocks*
  1 When the huge wave came, what happened to David?
  2 What did David hold on to?
  3 How did he get from the small island to Mull?
  4 What happened to his money?

9 *The lad with the silver button*
  1 Why didn't the old man see Alan's hat?
  2 Who was "the lad with the silver button"?
  3 Why didn't David understand the people of Mull?
  4 Why did David want to talk to Neil Roy?

10 *The "Red Fox" dies*
  1 Where, in Appin, did David land?
  2 Who was the red-haired man?
  3 What happened to him?
  4 Why did David start running up the hill?
  5 Why did the lawyer say "He's one of them"?

11 *James of the Glens*
  1 Who was the chieftain of the Campbells?
  2 Why was there a light in James Stewart's house?
  3 What was his wife doing?
  4 Who gave David some clothes?

12 *In the heather*
  1 What were the redcoats in the valley watching?
  2 Why did Alan and David leave the top of the rock?
  3 Where were they when they saw the dragoons?
  4 Where did they go to escape from the dragoons?

13 *The lawyer*
    1 Why couldn't they go across the bridge at Stirling?
    2 How did they cross the Firth of Forth?
    3 Who did David go to see?
    4 Why did Mr Rankeillor call Alan Breck "Mr Thomson"?
    5 Who did Ebenezer want to marry when he was young?

14 *Shaws is mine*
    1 What did Alan shout to Ebenezer?
    2 How much did Ebenezer pay Hoseason to kidnap David?
    3 How was Hoseason going to get more money?
    4 What did Rankeillor's clerk go to Shaws to do?

Questions on the whole story

These are harder questions. Read the Introduction, and think
hard about the questions before you answer them. Some of
them ask for your opinion, and there is no fixed answer.

1 Which of these people were (i) Jacobites, (ii) Whigs?
    a David Balfour
    b Alan Breck Stewart
    c Mr Campbell of Essendean
    d Colin of Glenure (the Red Fox)
    e James Stewart (James of the Glens)

2 If Robert Louis Stevenson had been alive in 1751, do you think
he would have been (i) a Jacobite or (ii) a Whig? Can you give
a reason for your answer?

3 Who was
    a "a small, unhealthy-looking man, about sixty years old" in
    Shaws?
    b "a fine tall gentleman, not like the rough hard man [David]
    had expected from Ransome's stories"?
    c "a smallish man, but strong-looking ... His face was dark
    from the sun, and his eyes were unusually light, with a kind
    of dancing fearlessness in them"?
    d "a great, red-headed man, very important-looking"?

4 Find these spoken words in the book, and answer the
  questions about them.

  a "Well, you can put it down outside the door, and go away."
    1 Who was the speaker?
    2 Who was he speaking to?
    3 What did he mean by "it"?
    4 What was the answer to the words?

  b "There are the twenty-pounders. They really are unhappy.
    And there are the children too."
    1 Who was the speaker?
    2 Who was he speaking to?
    3 What did he mean by "the twenty-pounders"?
    4 Who were "the children"?

  c "Am I not a bonny fighter?"
    1 Who was the speaker?
    2 Where was he?
    3 Who was he speaking to?
    4 What did he mean?
    5 What had he done?

  d "We will call your friend 'Mr Thomson', please, if by chance
    he is a Highlander."
    1 Who was the speaker?
    2 Where was he?
    3 Who was he speaking to?
    4 Who was the "friend"?
    5 What reason did the speaker give for using that name?
    6 Do you think it was the real reason?
    7 If it wasn't the real reason, why do you think he said it?

5 The last words of the story are: "into my house". Does it seem
  a good ending to you? Can you give reasons for your
  answer?

New words

bonny
(*Scots*) pretty; **a bonny fighter** = a man who fights well

chieftain
(*Scots*) the head of a **clan**

clan
(*Scots*) a large family; **clansman** = one (person) of a clan

cutlass
a kind of sword that is curved instead of straight

deck
the wooden floor over a ship

dragoons
soldiers with guns and heavy swords on horseback

firth
(*Scots*) a place where a river becomes wider as it comes to the sea

Gaelic
the Scots form of the language of the Celts, spoken in Britain before the arrival of English

heather
a plant found as small bushes covering open windy land (e.g. the Highlands of Scotland), with small flowers in summer

jury
a group of ordinary people (not lawyers or judges) who hear what is said in a trial and decide what the true facts are

kidnap
take someone away unlawfully to get money

kilt
a short skirt worn by Scotsmen, usually of **tartan** cloth

lad
a boy or young man; **lass** = a girl or young woman

laird
(*Scots*) a lord; landowner

pistol
a small gun to hold in one hand

plaid
(*Scots*) a long piece of woollen cloth usually carried over the shoulder

porridge
a breakfast food made with oats (a kind of grain) and water

shelter
a place where one finds cover from wind, rain, storms or enemies

spoilt
(especially of children) given so much that they think only about themselves and what they want, and not about other people

tartan
(*Scots*) woollen cloth with crossing lines of colour in an arrangement that is different for each clan